MARTHA

A PREQUEL TO THE STATIONMASTER'S COTTAGE

PHILLIPA NEFRI CLARK

PHILLIPA NEFRI CLARK
Mystery. Love. Suspense

Martha

Cover design by Steam Power Studios

Editing by Nas Dean

Martha is written in Australian English

ALSO BY PHILLIPA NEFRI CLARK

Christie Ryan Romantic Mysteries series

The Stationmaster's Cottage

Jasmine Sea

The Secrets of Palmerston House

The Christmas Key

Christie Ryan Romantic Mystery Boxed Set

Doctor Grok's Peculiar Shop (Paranormal Suspense shorts)

Colony

Table for Two

Wishing Well

Coming Soon

Last Known Contact

1

BENEATH THE WAVES

1972

Dark.

Dark, silent place.

But warm. Weightless warmth around me.

I'm sinking. Pulled down from the surface.

A single flash of light and I see where I am. Bubbles escape my mouth as I begin a scream but then my brain takes control. I clamp my lips together and get my bearings as the light shudders and fades.

Sand beneath my feet. Huge wooden pylons surround me. I'm under the jetty.

I stretch my arms upwards but my body won't follow. Something grips my waist. My dress is caught on a pylon nail and I'm not strong enough to pull free.

Utter quiet. Eyes sting. Air escapes my nose. My fault.

I've done this.

Around my face, my hair floats. Long hair and long dress. Floating.

Lightning again. And he is here beneath the waves. His eyes beg me to hold on as he nears and I reach for his hands.

His fingers. Mine. They touch.

I sigh in relief. Bubbles surround me as air leaves my lungs and when the sheet of light returns, I smile at him. Thomas fades to nothing.

2

GONE TOO SOON

1972

Martha gazed into the mirror in the hotel room. She didn't know how long she'd stood there, but her bare feet were freezing on the tiles, and steam from the shower had cleared from the glass. The sad green eyes staring back were not her own. Surely not. Tiredness formed lines on her forehead and around her mouth.

Too many bad dreams.

She sighed and reached for the solitary, threadbare towel. No wonder she was cold, standing here in an unheated bathroom with not even a dressing gown to warm her damp skin. As she dried her hair, Martha returned to the open suitcase on the bed. She had nothing suitable to wear and would need to find a dress shop somewhere before leaving for the funeral. She'd not thought it through in her rush to get here.

Travelling light meant exactly that. One suitcase contained much of her world. And her world wasn't geared for the loss of a parent.

If only she'd visited last year. And the year before. Or picked up a phone on his birthday. But weren't fathers supposed to always be there? It didn't matter that he was the one who'd left first. Not by much, but he and Mother had abandoned almost everything in the town she knew as home, only to move across the world.

Here in Ireland, the birthplace of Patrick Ryan's forefathers, he would be laid to rest. No doubt his funeral would be followed by a wake every bit as joyful and drunken as he so often was. Martha's lips curved upwards. The happiest drunk alive. At least back in Australia.

A glance at the clock beside the bed dragged Martha from her musings. She threw on brown slacks, a soft jumper she'd found at a market, and the short leather boots she'd taken everywhere since she left Australia. Once her hair was pulled back in a ponytail, she was presentable enough to shop for a dress she'd need to find space for in the bottom of the suitcase.

One day she'd find her home. A place and purpose just for her. Not yet though. No, not until the dreams left her alone.

She'd been right about the wake. Almost midnight, and the party continued. Cries of 'to Patrick', and 'gone but never forgotten', filled the house which Mother would now sell. It was nowhere as grand as Palmerston House, the home of Martha's childhood, now boarded up in the tiny seaside town of River's End. But perfect for her father. Close to pubs, near the sea, and with a new family of friends.

Lilian Ryan did and said all the right things. Even at this hour, after seeing her husband buried, her strict upbringing kept her focused. Her back was straight and her eyes clear as person after person commiserated or reminisced.

Mother never wanted help, let alone comfort. Even when Martha arrived at the house an hour before they needed to leave for the funeral, Lilian merely offered her tea and spoke of the weather. Only once was there an inkling of a crack in her shell. Just before they left.

"Is she running late?" Lilian had checked the window for the third time.

"Mother?" Martha's heart sank, hoping against hope her mother wasn't talking about Dorothy.

But she was. "Shouldn't your sister be here? Perhaps her flight was delayed. Or she couldn't get a taxi to bring her this far. Oh, I should have arranged someone to meet her—"

"Dorothy isn't coming." Martha enfolded her mother in her arms, wishing she'd stop hoping. For an instant, Lilian's shoulders dropped, but then she stepped away from Martha's embrace.

"I see."

"Dorothy should be here. There's no 'I see' about it." Martha had crossed her arms. "She had time and she certainly has the money for the airfare."

Lilian had shrugged and walked away. "I'll fetch my purse."

And now they were at the end of the wake. Drunk men and sympathetic women spilled out onto the driveway, until at last the house was quiet. Martha locked the front door and collected the last of the plates. In the kitchen, Lilian stood at the sink, fingers in the water, eyes closed.

How will she cope?

As much as her parents disagreed on almost everything, their love was true. Enduring. And now Daddy was gone forever and nothing would ever be the same. Whatever that meant.

"I'll finish this, Mother. You go to bed."

With a nod, Lilian opened her eyes, then dried her hands on a tea towel. "Will you stay a while, child?"

"I…I can't. There's only one bus and I'll miss the connection to London if I don't leave first thing. I'm sorry."

Lilian took Martha's hand and squeezed it. There were tears in her eyes. Martha swallowed to push down a sympathetic rush of emotion.

"You're a good girl, Martha. And I made a terrible mistake."

"Mother?"

"I think it was my fault. I should have accepted…him."

An icy shiver ran down Martha's spine. "Who?"

"Your Thomas. He wasn't a bad boy. I'd just forgotten what young love felt like." Lilian kissed Martha's cheek. "I'm going to bed."

Lilian released Martha's hand and shuffled to the door, exhaustion in every step. She'd aged in front of Martha today. The strong woman, opinionated and unafraid was buried beneath a quiet grief. But what she'd said spun around Martha's mind.

"How was any of it your fault, Mother?" Martha caught up with her. "He chose someone else."

"Things are never as they seem, child. Goodnight."

"What do you mean?" But Lilian was gone, her heavy footsteps slowly heading to the staircase.

3

ALONE

1972

Passengers chatted as the old bus rattled over yet another bridge. Martha rubbed her hands together, wishing she'd bought gloves.

A cup of tea with Lilian early this morning, before daylight forced its way through heavy mist, was strained and quick. Her mother looked as though she'd cried all night. Barely a word passed her lips and when Martha asked what she'd meant about Thomas and Dorothy, all she got was the shake of her head.

Only when Martha picked up her suitcase near the front door did Lilian grasp her arm, eyes wide.

"Move here. Please, child."

"Here? But I'm studying for another year in England."

"Can't you transfer to Ireland? We're not so far from Dublin and you could live here and wouldn't need to work."

The bus pulled over to let a stream of cars pass. Martha stared out of the rain-streaked window at the grey sea. Nothing like River's End, where the ocean went on forever beneath a deep blue sky. Where she was born and raised and where she belonged.

Where I once belonged.

Another year and she'd be a teacher. Not the future she'd once imagined but a practical and satisfying career. Mother did understand, but was alone and afraid and for that, Martha hurt. She wished she'd had more time to stay. Mother should return to Australia, to Palmerston House. At least she had friends there and would be closer to Dorothy.

With a jolt, the bus got going. It needed to make up time if she was to reach Dublin before the boat left.

There was no point worrying about Mother. When Martha needed her most, she and Dad simply upped and left the country. What was meant to be a long holiday in the country of his ancestors became permanent.

And neither she nor Dorothy were consulted. Just informed that Palmerston House would remain boarded up indefinitely until they decided what to do with it.

Dorothy had been furious. She'd stomped around her apartment in Melbourne shouting about the responsibilities always put on her shoulders. The next day, Martha had packed her small collection of clothes. She had waited until Dorothy returned from work and quietly said her goodbyes.

The last words she heard from her older sister was as she had abruptly shut the door behind Martha. "Don't expect me to fix this when it all goes wrong."

She had pulled her shoulders back, held her head high and by the time she had descended to the ground floor, all the tears were wiped away. Martha had stepped out onto the evening street in Melbourne and never looked back.

Her past was in Australia, and soon, Ireland. Father was gone, Dorothy didn't care, and Thomas… Martha's fingers curled around each other.

"I should have accepted him. He wasn't a bad boy." That's what Mother had said last night.

"Then why didn't you?" Martha whispered.

The woman in the next seat glanced at her. Martha looked out of the window again, avoiding her own eyes reflecting back in the glass. Outside, the sky was brighter, the rain stopped. The bus slowed as they entered a village, then stopped to let a group of school children cross. Their laughter made Martha smile. They waved at the bus and she waved back until they ran through the gate of a tiny primary school.

One day she'd be a teacher, waiting for her class to arrive. Nurturing young minds and hearts and helping them reach for their dreams. Probably in London, where demand was high. As the road went up a hill, Martha might have been back in River's End. Curved, narrow roads, the sea, and small town folk.

Perhaps there were jobs for teachers in towns like this. She'd be close enough to Mother to keep an eye on her, but far enough away to still have a relationship with her. And far enough away from River's End to keep the heartache at bay.

4

MARTHA'S COTTAGE

1977

It was hers.

Martha braced herself against the icy wind flying off the Atlantic Ocean to run to the front gate for the third time in an hour. Snuggled into a heavy jacket, a scarf controlling most of her hair, she couldn't stop grinning.

At the little iron gate, she turned. The white stone cottage smiled back at her. It knew she was about to transform it from a worn out, unloved house into a warm and pretty home. To anyone else, it was overgrown, in need of some basic repairs, and too far out of town to be bothered with.

The last point wasn't quite true, it actually was only a ten-minute walk. Martha loved the idea of walking to work every day, even in the cold. And at the worst, the school bus could collect her along its route.

Between the gate and the front door, grass grew through a brick path. On either side were the remains of narrow garden beds. Well, she'd be planting some bright and pretty flowers once she found out what grew here.

A particularly strong gust of wind shook the gate and Martha glanced behind. Across the road was a wide grass verge and then a rocky descent to a pebbled beach. Not quite the white expanse of soft sand she was used to, but it would do. The sky was heavy with rain clouds and as they scuttled her way, Martha scampered inside, closing the red door behind her with some effort.

She'd moved in two days ago and had so little, but it didn't matter. The fireplace was lit and warmth radiated through the room which was part living area and part dining, with a cosy kitchen looking over the sea. The kitchen was dominated by a wood stove which she'd already discovered was cantankerous.

There was an old fridge but she had ordered a new one from Dublin, along with a bed to replace the quite horrible one in the larger of two bedrooms.

"If I can sleep comfortably and stock up on fresh food then there is little else I urgently need." She'd told the realtor, who'd shrugged. He was relieved to sell, from what she could tell, and wasn't local. The cottage was last owned by an elderly woman who'd been moved into care in the city and it was her family who wanted it sold.

Martha peered out through the windows. "Well, I shall love you as she once did. And never leave you."

That said, she opened the last of her boxes from England, emptying the contents onto the heavy timber dining table. Since arriving in London six years ago, she'd collected enough to live on, but not enough to hold her to one place. And she'd moved often, particularly the first couple of years, living more out of her suitcase than anything.

This box followed her from Australia. Dorothy grew tired of holding onto items Martha forgot to pack when she left and tracked her down in London. After one look inside, Martha taped it up and never opened it again. Until now.

When Mother and Dorothy had persuaded her to spend time in Melbourne, she'd packed with no interest in the future. Her world had crashed around her and it was Dorothy who eventually took over, gathering a selection of Martha's possessions.

From her desk at Palmerston House was a framed photograph of the family when Martha was ten. She remembered the day well, as Father had made non-stop jokes about the camera stealing his soul. She touched his face with trembling fingers.

There was a bunch of letters tied up with string, all from Dorothy, written after she left Palmerston House to begin her life in the city. It was soon after the family photos were taken, and kept Martha close to her big sister. For a while, anyway.

A bundle of paperbacks was a welcome find. Reading something other than exam papers and timetables was such a pleasant thought.

At the bottom was a small jewellery box. Martha picked it up, her heart racing. It would be silly to open it. Why make herself sad? And yet, she suddenly wanted to see it again.

Inside the box was a gold pendant. Two letters—T and M—entwined. The chain was fragile and perfect. "Oh, Thomas."

Her hands shook and she closed the lid, then shoved it into the box. She replaced the tape the best she could. There was a cupboard near the back door and Martha pushed the box into the bottom, behind a broom and mop.

She was so cold. The fire was all but out and the sun completely gone. Martha's heart yearned for another time, another place. But, this was her home now. Her little school was depending upon her. This cottage needed her.

One day she might take the pendant out and wear it. One day, her emotions might settle to a fond memory of the man she loved beyond life. Not today though.

5

LOST FOREVER

1980

His arms are around me.

I lean back against his bare chest to listen to the familiar, dear sound of his heartbeat again. We've been apart for too long.

A moment apart is too long.

Thomas loves me and we are together. This time nobody will get between us.

The hammock we lay on in the sun swings with a warm breeze off the sea. Back and forth. We've been here for hours, days. I don't remember when we arrived and I don't want to leave this place. The sun is so nice, so…

It disappears behind a cloud. No, not a cloud. A wave, roaring across the white sand, towering above me. White foam mixed with dark water crashes over me and I am wrenched from Thomas' arms, dragged over the sand, sucked into the sea.

Now I float beneath the surface, carried this way and that by the tug of the tide. Thomas will find me. He always does and then we will swim to the cool air above.

Like a stone, I sink. I'm on the sand at the bottom of the sea and it is dark.

There is nothing here.

6

FAILING TO MOVE ON

1980

The night sky was lightening. Sunrise wasn't far away. Martha slowly extricated herself from the arms holding her. It was time to leave.

In the tiny bathroom, Martha dressed and washed her face. Enrique stirred as she let herself out so she watched as he settled back into sleep. She ran down the flight of stairs to the street, and stopped long enough to draw in the already warm dawn air. The dream followed her along the narrow streets of Lima, troubling her senses.

The humidity was as stifling as the air that night in River's End. Martha hurried to the edge of the city where almost sheer cliffs dropped to narrow roads and the ocean. The scent fuelled the memories of stormy seas churning. But the sea here washed in calmly.

How do I let this go?

She stood near the edge of the cliff, clutching her handbag and swaying in time with the tide. It soothed her. Reminded her of happier days sitting at the end of the jetty with Thomas, laughing and basking in his love.

Lips curving up, she sighed. He'd been her world. No matter what happened at the end, Thomas remained the one who possessed her heart. She might as well accept it and move on. Yet every time she tried, the dreams would haunt her nights.

With a last look at the sea, Martha turned. Her hotel was not far and she longed for a shower and change of clothes. This was her third visit to Peru and would be her last. Enrique had kept her coming back here. Until now.

Martha waited outside the hotel for the taxi. She still travelled light, her old suitcase replaced by one more modern but surprisingly sturdy. The day was as sticky and humid as she'd expected and the cooler days of Ireland beckoned her home. School would start soon.

The taxi pulled up.

"Martha! Wait." Enrique sprinted toward her. He carried her light jacket in one hand, something she'd not even noticed missing when she packed. The driver took her suitcase to put in the boot.

"*Por favor espero?*" she asked the driver and he nodded. No doubt he was used to tourists wanting to stop and admire the scenery of his city.

Enrique grinned widely as he reached her, panting. "You… left…this."

She took it from him. "You didn't need to run all this way. But thank you."

He drew in a long breath. "Martha. I would have kept it safe. For next visit."

Martha dropped her gaze.

"Is okay. I know there won't be another."

Her eyes shot back to his. They'd been friends for a long time after meeting at a nightclub in Los Angeles on one of her school breaks. He'd offered to teach her to cook chili at his restaurant in Peru so she'd visited the following year. And kept returning.

"What do you mean?" Her voice trembled. She hadn't even fully decided. Who knew where the trade winds would take her next?

Enrique took her hands in his. "*Pequeño amor,* you always say goodbye. Not leave before dawn without coffee."

"I…I didn't wish to wake you so early."

He lifted her hands and kissed them one at a time, eyes never leaving hers. "Thomas is a lucky man. To have your heart. It is time for you to find him."

Tears stung Martha's eyes and she blinked rapidly. He must have heard her call out from her bad dream.

"Or, you could stay." A flash of sadness crossed his face, then he smiled. "You don't need to answer, *mi amor*. Have a safe return."

"Enrique…"

"Your driver waits. Maybe we meet again. And dance under starlight." He released her hands.

"I hope so."

As the taxi drove down the road she watched Enrique until he was out of sight, and then the tears came.

7

VISITORS

1982

Halfway up the hill to her cottage, Martha crossed to the ocean side of the road as she did most days. With winter approaching, the otherwise pleasant day was already cooling, and the nights came early. But the sky was clear and deep blue. Far out to sea, light reflected off a ship. A cargo ship. Closer to shore, sailboats dotted the sea.

The breeze picked up and Martha rubbed her bare arms. Time to get home and bring some wood inside. Between the stove and the fireplace, she was continually loading her barrow from the shed up the back. One more glance at the view and she hurried back over the road.

Once the wood was in and stacked, she'd get the stove working and throw some vegetables in a pot to simmer for soup. It'll cook whilst she marked exam papers. Such a fun part of her job, with cute notes some students added for her. She'd promised the mixed class of students they'd have their results tomorrow.

With a smile, she picked up her pace. As she reached the crest of the hill, she slowed again, puzzled at the car parked outside her gate. Her visitors came on foot, or bicycle as a rule. The car was empty but voices from near her front door drifted over.

"I'm happy to drive you back later." A male voice she didn't recognise.

"No, I'll wait. Sooner or later that school must finish for the day."

Mother?

The gate squeaked as Martha opened it. Lilian waited near the front door beside a man in his sixties. They looked up and Lilian stepped toward her with a smile. Had she been holding the man's hand?

"Darling. We thought you'd never get home." Lilian kissed Martha's cheek. "They are working you too hard, child. You look so tired."

"Um, thanks. Hi." Martha sized up the man. A bit taller than Lilian, which made him not quite Martha's height, he had a cheery expression and red hair. He offered his hand.

"Seamus Foley, and it is nice to finally meet you, Miss Martha."

"Just Martha is fine, please."

She glanced from Seamus to her mother. They exchanged a look and Martha's stomach tightened. "Please, come in. I'll make some tea. Or coffee." Martha unlocked the door and gestured for them to enter.

Inside, Lilian gazed around with her lips pursed.

Stop being so judgemental, Mother!

The cottage might not be as grand as Palmerston House, or large as Mother's house in town, but it was renovated to create a warm and inviting interior. Thick rugs covered much of the stone floor, a comfortable sofa sat opposite two armchairs, and the scent of flowers filled the room from vases of roses. The kitchen was still old—traditional if one wanted to sound like a realtor, but apart from the stove had modern appliances and was spotless.

"Tea? Or coffee?" Martha filled the kettle. She wasn't about to let Mother annoy her.

"Oh, tea is fine. Seamus has his white with two sugars. Shall we sit?"

"Of course. Please make yourselves at home and I won't be long."

By the time Martha carried a tray laden with a teapot, cups and saucers, and some slices of a fruit pie from the fridge, she'd talked herself into staying calm. Whatever brought Mother here, she needed to listen, not react.

Seamus took some pie, but Lilian insisted she was watching her weight. As if she needed to. If anything, Lilian was on the thin side, and when Martha looked more closely, she saw new lines in her mother's face. What did she expect? Mother was in her sixties now.

For a while, they chatted about Martha's work at the school, the weather, and politics. Seamus helped himself to more pie and said little, but smiled often at Lilian.

"Anyway, there is a reason for our visit today. Apart from not seeing you for months on end."

"It was only…well, okay. Sorry."

"What matters is now. I hope you'll be as happy as I am when you hear my news." Lilian glanced at Seamus and reached for his hand. "Our news."

Stay calm. Breathe.

Lilian continued, her eyes suddenly bright and a smile turning her face young again. "Seamus has asked me to marry him, and I've said I would be honoured."

But...Daddy.

Martha gripped her bottom lip so hard with her teeth it hurt.

"Darling? Please don't be upset. It means a lot to me." Never had Lilian's voice been so pleading, so soft.

"I'm…I'm not, Mother. It just surprised me. Congratulations. To you both."

"I promise I'll treat your Mum well." Seamus leaned forward. "She'll have a happy life."

"She had a happy life with Daddy." Martha jumped up and began collecting cups. "I'm sorry. I didn't mean to say it that way." She looked at her mother. "I am pleased for you, Mother, really I am."

"You don't sound it!" Lilian got to her feet, her face red. "Patrick passed away more than ten years ago, child. Ten sad, lonely years. And

I miss him even now." Seamus stood and put an arm around her shoulders. "But he'd want me to go on. And I thought you would too."

"I want you to be happy, Mother. It just never occurred to me you'd find someone else."

Lilian reached for her handbag. "Just because you refuse to accept the truth about Thomas and live your life to its fullest, doesn't mean other people can't."

Martha gasped and put a hand to her mouth.

"Look at yourself, Martha. Living in this little place alone. Walking to work. No love in your life. Not even bothering to visit your own mother on a regular basis." Lilian sniffed and stalked to the front door, Seamus hurrying behind her. "I'll send you an invitation to our wedding of course. Perhaps by then you'll have got over yourself."

Heat rushed from Martha's toes to the top of her head, forcing her into action. As Seamus opened the door, she reached her mother. "Invite Dorothy. Invite your favourite daughter. She might not disappoint you."

"Oh, ladies, no." Seamus frowned. "I didn't mean to make trouble and I think you should both take a breath and say sorry."

Sorry is the last thing I'll say!

Lilian's eyes narrowed and whatever she'd been about to reply was kept to herself. Martha knew her well enough to see the struggle behind the forced smile. It was many years since they'd had words and the old feelings of being the lesser child rose.

"We'll send you an invitation, Martha. Thank you for your hospitality." Lilian leaned forward and kissed Martha's cheek, then walked out.

Martha couldn't even watch her go. She closed the door, locked it, and leaned back against it to support herself, so hard were her legs shaking. Nothing ever changed with Mother.

8

TOO LATE TO SAY SORRY

1983

Both front and back doors of the cottage were wide open. First day of spring meant spring cleaning to Martha and she took it seriously. She'd dragged the small rugs outdoors after dawn, hauling them over the low stone walls around the garden and beating them senseless. The curtains weighed down the clothes line, and now she worked on the window panes.

This was the fifth year she'd done this and as hard work as it was, she knew she'd reach evening and be satisfied with a sparkling home again, ready for the warmer months.

Once the windows were done, she took everything off the mantelpiece to clean it.

"Oh."

Behind the clock was an envelope with embossed gold writing. Mother and Seamus' wedding invitation. She'd forgotten it was there and glanced at the card inside. Three weeks until the big day, and the RSVP was tomorrow. Martha put the envelope on the kitchen table and poured a glass of water.

Despite several civil phone conversations with Lilian, Martha had not seen her since their argument last year. Not even for Christmas, even though Lilian invited her over. She'd made excuses about having another commitment, somewhere else to be, yet had spent Christmas Eve and Christmas Day as she always did. Alone in the cottage.

Was Dorothy going to attend? She hadn't come for Daddy's funeral so would she be bothered to travel across the globe for a wedding? If she didn't, then Mother had no family to attend. Martha sighed. She was getting too old to hold onto grudges. Of course she'd be there for Mother.

She dialled Mother's number but it rang out. Martha hung up the phone and returned to the cleaning. She'd try again tonight.

A glass of sherry was in order after such a productive day. Martha wandered around the cottage as she sipped, as pleased with the result of her labour as she'd known she'd be. The fireplace was ready to be lit, but as the sun set, the cottage was still warm enough to wait a while.

Outside, a car door shut. Martha's heart raced. If this was Mother, then she needed to be sure she wouldn't lose her temper again. She left her glass in the kitchen and peered out. It was a police car. How strange. They were several towns away from a police station. Two police officers came through the gate and she met them at the front door.

"Miss Ryan?" The older man nodded as he introduced himself and his partner but Martha didn't register the names. The expression on his face froze her in place.

"Shall we step indoors? We have some bad news for you."

She never knew how she ended up sitting on the sofa, the police officer patting her shoulder as tears streamed down her face. His partner emerged from the kitchen with a cup of tea which she took, but couldn't drink.

"Are...are you sure?" A last grab for a way out of this nightmare.

"Very sure, I'm afraid. Both your mother and Mr Foley were confirmed on the boat. Six souls lost to the sea. Is there someone we can call? A relative, friend?"

It was hours later when Martha managed to dial Australia, her fingers still shaking, her head throbbing. When Dorothy answered, Martha blurted out the terrible news, then burst into tears again. To a stony silence, she explained about a small chartered boat to celebrate the upcoming wedding amongst six friends. A freak wave in unseasonably rough seas.

"You should never have let her on a boat!" Dorothy screamed down the line.

"I didn't know."

"This is unbearable. Lost to the sea. Oh, why? Why must this never end?"

"Dorothy, I don't understand. Will you come to help with the funeral? With the house?"

But Dorothy refused. She was too busy with her business, she said. If everyone would have stayed in Australia, this wouldn't have happened. And then she hung up.

There'd been no wake for Mother. Hers was the last of the six funerals. Martha attended Seamus' a day earlier, standing back as she wasn't his family and had not allowed him to become her friend. He'd been nice, had loved Mother, so one day they would have forged a relationship.

Lilian Ryan was laid to rest alongside Patrick. Unbeknown to Lilian, he'd bought two plots not long after they relocated to Ireland, so here was where Martha felt it was right to bury her mother. She might have moved on in life, but Patrick was the man she'd loved for decades and now death reunited them.

As death will one day reunite me with Thomas.

But Thomas wasn't dead, and for all Martha knew, he may not

ever think about her, let alone want to see her in any afterlife there might be.

I still love you though, and always will.

The drive home was surreal. Perfect spring weather. Children playing outside their houses. People greeting one another in the streets. Mother would never see another day. She'd miss her own wedding. Martha had lost the chance to say sorry, to put things right and support her mother with a happy heart.

She stepped into the cottage and slipped off her shoes. Her mother had been right that day. Martha didn't live her life to the fullest, despite her travels and occasional relationships. It was too late to think of a husband and children now. But there was a whole world of experiences out there waiting.

Martha opened the cupboard by the back door and took out the box she'd left there for years. She held up the pendant, the T and M entwined. This time she smiled, and then opened the clasp and put the chain around her neck.

9

FRIENDS FOREVER

1985

Nothing, but nothing Martha had ever experienced prepared her for this. The Lofoten Islands in Norway was the destination she'd expected when she'd planned this remote trip, but here she was, miles further out on a small fishing boat. She did, after all, know its owner, who was inside getting hot mead to warm their hands as much as their stomachs as they closed in on the anchor point.

Aksel.

Martha couldn't help smiling. They'd met in Ireland in her local pub when he took a year away from work to discover the world. His stories of life in Norway, the endless sea and incredible sky, was enough to send her looking for places to stay. How he'd teased her about what she considered icy conditions when the wind off the Atlantic Ocean shook her cottage.

"Visit me. And shop first for proper clothing. I'll make a list."

And he had. The holiday was two years in the making, and the journey itself challenging, with transport from plane to train, bus to foot, and boats.

Ten people were along tonight. Or was it day? This time of year they looked the same, so far north. It was cold in a way Ireland wasn't. Not always wind or snow, but a deep coldness that cut into you. Martha shivered and tucked her scarf in a bit more. The boat was an hour from land and the sea quite choppy, but she didn't care. She loved the ocean as much as she always had, despite nearly losing her own life in it once, and losing her mother to it.

"Are you English?" A soft female voice made Martha turn. The woman beside her was younger, a classically beautiful face with strikingly sad eyes.

"Australian, actually. But I live in Ireland."

"I'm Elizabeth White. My husband is somewhere around. He loves the sea." Elizabeth smiled.

"So do I. And you are English."

"I'm afraid the accent gives it away every time."

"And a lovely one it is." Aksel returned, handing Martha a steaming cup. "There's plenty inside, Mrs White, which is where I just saw your husband."

"I might join him then. Nice to meet you…"

"Martha. Martha Ryan."

When Elizabeth disappeared inside, Aksel dropped a kiss onto Martha's forehead. "Alone at last."

"Apart from ten other tourists and your staff."

Aksel shrugged. "Drink up. And, you might want to turn around, but don't drop your cup."

As if she would do such a thing. Martha turned to look over the side of the boat. And gasped.

Above her, the black sky morphed into a thousand moving colours. A curtain of a million stars hosted the light show, a slowly moving kaleidoscope of green, blue, and gold. Swirls and waterfalls of colour filled the sky.

Joy and delight and terror mingled inside Martha until she began to cry soft, silent tears that almost froze as they fell from her eyes. Aksel surrounded her with his strong arms and gently tilted her face this way, then that, to take in every detail of the Northern Lights. Aurora Borealis at its finest.

"I…oh, Aksel."

He chuckled. "Tourist."

Martha laughed aloud. "That I am! How do you get anything done living here?"

"Being in the dark half the year, you don't see the neglect. Haven't painted the boat in years, or the house." He laughed again. "Grew up with it, but still, it amazes me."

"Wow. Keith, look!" Elizabeth was beside them, this time with a tall, slender man holding her arm. Her face was alight with the same wonder Martha knew must be on her own, yet those eyes still haunted her with their sadness.

Many hours later, as the boat headed back to the town, Martha and Elizabeth wandered alone around the boat. Everyone else was inside, away from the increasingly freezing conditions, but they were arm in arm, each with another of Aksel's spiced drinks.

They stopped at the stern, gazing at the Northern Lights.

"It almost made me cry." Elizabeth said.

"It definitely made me cry!"

"Oh, did it?" Elizabeth sipped her drink. "Lately, I'm all cried out."

Martha turned her back on the lights to give Elizabeth her full attention. "I feel as though I've known you forever." She tilted her head.

Elizabeth nodded. "As do I. And I'm sure it is the mead, and the scenery, and perhaps the cold, but I do believe we will be friends always."

"I agree. And you must come to Ireland."

"We will. These few months are about us. You see, we found out we cannot…I cannot have children. It hurts."

Martha put her arms around Elizabeth and squeezed tightly. "I am so very, very sorry."

Approaching footsteps drew them apart. Martha whispered. "I shall never be married, so perhaps we shall both have adventures together?"

As though the telling helped her, the sadness lifted from Elizabeth's eyes, replaced with mirth. "And keep everyone on their toes! I should like that."

10

A MILESTONE

1987

Dear Martha,

Happy 40th Birthday. I do miss you.

Dorothy

Martha checked the envelope for more than a card with a flower on the outside, and Dorothy's perfect handwriting inside. Nothing else. No letter, or even a note.

I do miss you.

"Then visit me!" Martha sighed and took the card to the mantelpiece. The picture on the card was quite pretty, a single white tulip in a slim crystal vase. Something Dorothy might well have at home. All Dorothy ever talked about when they were growing up was having a beautiful home filled with precious objects. It was close to twenty years since they'd seen each other, but Martha doubted anything would have stopped her sister reaching her goals.

She'd collected her mail on the way in from school, juggling an assortment of presents from the students. The best news though was her promotion to principal. The retiring principal had been adamant

Martha was his perfect replacement, and the official notice had arrived this morning. When the students were informed, a cheer broke out. As firm as she was with them, they all knew she had a soft side and loved her as much as she adored each of them.

In an hour or so, a group of her friends were expecting her for dinner and celebrations at the pub. This village and its people were her family as much as anyone could be. Even the old-timers who treated anyone not from the region with suspicion had finally accepted her. It was a good place to live.

But forty years old! How had the time got away? Martha wandered outside to her back garden, her greatest joy. Here she cultivated vegetables and flowers, and crooked row of fruit trees. Every season there was something different to preserve or bottle, freeze or dry. She even entered her jams into the local show each year and was no stranger to winning awards.

Martha settled on a bench beneath one of the old trees. From here, the garden surrounded her, so alike the one around another home. Her fingers played with her pendant. The porch at the back of the stationmaster's cottage had a love seat, and there she'd sat many times with Thomas. Their hands entwined, they'd watch night fall over the long-established garden with its beautiful orchard behind the vegetable patch.

"I've made my own cottage here."

Alone.

No husband or children. Not even a pet, not with the amount of travelling she enjoyed. No Dorothy, and no Thomas.

Well, she had a busy, fulfilling life and friends. Speaking of which, she might go down to the pub a bit early and toast herself with whatever champagne they kept for special occasions.

11

GOOD MOTIVES. BAD CHOICES

1993

"I think the battery is going on this one." Martha tapped her flashlight and the beam flickered back on. "Or a loose connection."

"Which is another good reason to go back now." Elizabeth stopped walking and crossed her arms. "I don't believe it is even legal!"

Keith grinned as Martha turned back. "She does have a point, Martha. If you're not allowed on them during the day, odds are you aren't at night."

"I did ask."

"Since when did you speak fluent Egyptian? I think the poor man you asked had no idea what you were going on about. No, I think we should go and find some dinner in town." Elizabeth shook her head.

Martha glanced back into the dark. Rising from the sandy ground, the remains of a pyramid loomed above her. For the past week, she'd spent a wonderful time with Elizabeth and Keith, and this was their final night in Egypt.

"I'll tell you what," she smiled at Elizabeth. "Give me just five minutes so I can go up a few steps, that's all. I'll be right back. Okay?"

She didn't wait to hear a response. In a moment, she was taking careful steps up the side that was much steeper than she'd expected. No sprinting easily up mountains man-made or otherwise anymore. And she was being a bit cheeky by climbing onto the ancient relic even though her motives were pure. This school term she was teaching about the pyramids and all she wanted was a moment to explore, to touch, and absorb the wonder of the history.

As she crossed a gap between blocks the flashlight went out. Instead of stone, her foot met air and for one heart-stopping second she grappled for a handhold. The flashlight slipped from her fingers and she heard it hit the ground.

Her hands flapped wildly, missing any purchase, and she fell, tumbling from narrow step to narrow step, pain shooting through her hips and shoulders where she landed.

Eyes clenched shut, arms reaching up to protect her head, air forced from her lungs into a long, low cry, Martha heard the snap as her legs buckled. With a scream, she thudded onto her side.

"Martha!"

She lay winded, barely aware of gentle hands, of something covering her body. Her ankle was on fire. Everything hurt. Above her, huge stars blinked in silent reproach. *Stay off the pyramid.*

"Oh, darling. We'll get you to a hospital."

"Elizabeth, we'll need to splint it first. I'll find some help."

Keith must have left, but Elizabeth held her hand and made soothing sounds. Martha's breathing steadied and she lifted herself up a bit.

"Don't move too much, your ankle is broken I'm afraid." Elizabeth's face hovered near Martha's, lined with worry.

"I'm fine, just a little fall." Adrenalin pumped through Martha. The pain was a throb now, and thoughts rushed around her head. "You are the best friends ever. And the other day on the Nile when you said you were looking for a new start? Do you remember?"

"Well, yes, but you really should rest."

"Did you mean it when you said you'd love to move to Australia? Because I thought of something. About Palmerston House."

"Your family home?"

"It will stay boarded up forever unless someone buys it. And it isn't for sale because I don't think Dorothy wants to let it go. But if you spoke to her…not telling her it was my idea. It is big enough to become a bed and breakfast, like you wanted."

"We're almost there!" Keith's voice drifted from a distance.

"It sounds wonderful, Martha. But I think we might get you to hospital and then we'll discuss it later."

Martha nodded and lay back, moaning as pain radiated up her leg.

"I promise, we'll talk. After we discuss a no pyramid climbing policy." Elizabeth kissed Martha's cheek as Keith arrived.

Anything for you, my dear friend. Anything at all.

12

OUT OF REACH

2005

I'm on the jetty. The night air cools my face and the soft splosh of water against the pylons reminds me the tide is beginning to rise. Below my bare feet the old timber boards are rough, and they creak as I move to the very edge.

The water is clear and by the light of the full moon I see juvenile King Whiting swim this way and that around the seaweed on the sandy seabed. We've sat here so often, watching the fish and sunrise and sunset, and sometimes nothing at all but each other.

A hot wind lifts my long hair from my shoulders. I look down at the emerald green dress hugging my body, the bottom of the skirt touching my ankles. Tonight was our engagement party and I wore this, loving the soft fabric against my bare legs.

On my hand is my engagement ring, a solitaire. So perfect and beautiful. And I wear Tom's pendant. A gift from my twentieth birthday. But where is he?

I turn to scan the beach but it is so dark.

"Thomas?"

I walk back along the jetty and go to the sand, so hot beneath my feet. A wave rolls over my toes and I stay where I am, enjoying the water.

Lightning forks onto the cliff above the stone steps and I see him. Thomas walks away from me, his head down.

"Tom! I'm here!"

But he keeps walking. And now the waves are around my hips, then my waist, until one roars over my head and I am below the sea again.

13

AN UNFINISHED PLAN

2005

"Tom!" Martha's eyes flew open. Dawn was peeking through the windows. Windows with a view to the Atlantic Ocean, not the Great Southern Ocean where her heart belonged.

Unwanted tears dripped down her face as she gave in to the memories. Her beloved town of River's End, the friends she'd grown up with and a sister who'd once been loving and sweet. Two parents proud of their home and the life they'd created for their family. And Thomas Blake.

Gone forever.

She reached for tissues, sat up and blew her nose. This wasn't how women in their late fifties behaved. A school principal, no less. Yet, these dreams continued, even though they'd stopped being every night, or week, or month now.

It was time to get up, get moving, and get over the past. How she'd tried. And how many experiences she'd enjoyed in the process.

You should write a book.

Halfway out of bed, Martha stopped, mouth open. Something

stirred in her memories. A conversation with Tom when she'd been angry with him. Furious in fact. But it was her reply to him which struck a chord now. *"I want to travel the world. I want to be a famous writer."*

She shook her head, slid her feet into slippers, and wrapped a dressing gown around herself.

As the kettle heated, Martha prepared a teapot, glancing outside as the first rays of sun lit the sea. It was the middle of summer, not a long warm season as Australia offered, but a time she loved nevertheless.

There was a seat outside, a narrow bench against the stone wall. She sat there, nursing her hot cup and watching birds begin their day-long hunt for food.

She had travelled much of the world. Most of Europe, North and South America, and parts of Asia. The world was more familiar than her birth place. So she'd accomplished one of her declared intentions and how wonderful the memories were.

Over the years she'd kept notes, diaries of sorts, with photos and memorabilia from the most treasured places. Even Egypt.

Martha glanced at her ankle. At the hospital she'd pressured the doctor into setting the injury for her flight home the next day. He'd advised her to wait for a few days, let the swelling subside and full x-rays be done, but she needed to come home. The ankle set, and she recovered, but it was never the same. A lasting reminder not to do the wrong thing, even for the right reason.

Her life was busy and fulfilling so becoming a famous writer wasn't on the horizon. Maybe one day, when she retired, she'd think about turning those memories into something. For now though, she had garden beds to weed, seedlings to plant, and fruit to bottle.

"Mornin' Miss!"

A group of children ran past, waving as they crossed the road to go down to the beach. Martha waved back. She had these youngsters to teach and every year brought a sense of happiness almost nothing else could. Her hand went to her pendant. Almost.

14

A PROD FROM A FRIEND

2007

Martha's birthday came and went quietly. No doubt her friends in the village would have made a big deal of it had she reminded them it was her sixtieth, but for some reason, she wanted to keep the day to herself.

The morning had passed in its usual Saturday way with housekeeping, some gardening, and a few cups of her favourite tea. Then, she'd dressed in her best dress and taken the bus to Dublin where she'd shouted herself lunch at a fancy restaurant. Every bite was delicious, and there was a certain pleasure in eating alone and being waited upon.

On a whim, she joined the queue of mostly families with younger children to see a new film. Who could resist the tale of a lonely boy and an unusual egg set in a part of Scotland she adored? She'd spent many hours herself at Loch Ness, waiting in hope for a glimpse of the creature she really wanted to believe in. The film was delightful, even if she'd had to use a few tissues part way through.

But worth every moment.

Martha arrived home near dark, the bus driver kindly stopping near her gate. By now, her ankle throbbed, so she was relieved to go inside and take off her shoes. She giggled as she changed into pyjamas and dressing gown for the rest of the evening.

From the city she'd brought a selection of cheese, a bottle of Australian wine, and some lovely bread. This simple meal rounded off what was a wonderful day. And then, there were the presents!

One by one, she opened the small pile of gifts which had arrived at the cottage, and from school, over the past week. A couple of new release novels, which she immediately put to one side to look at before bed. From her students, a pretty scarf from a local shop. The teachers sent a bottle of her favourite sherry and Waterford crystal glasses.

"Oh my, how very pretty!"

The last gift, the one she'd left to unwrap at the end, was from Elizabeth. Like an excited child, she tore off the wrapping and put the card to one side so she could see what Elizabeth had sent. Her hand flew to her mouth.

The final piece of wrapping paper floated to the ground, revealing a leather book. On the cover, engraved in gold, were the words "Martha's Adventures".

She opened it to Elizabeth's beautiful handwriting.

"To my dearest friend who taught me to live life to the fullest."

This was a journal, ready for words. A small fire ignited deep in Martha.

She slid the card from its envelope.

Happy Birthday, darling Martha!

I miss you so much but imagine you happy and well in your dear cottage. This gift is to encourage you to record your wonderful travels and perhaps share them with the world.

All is well here in River's End and I love Palmerston House more with each passing year.

As ever,

Elizabeth

Her eyes suddenly misty, Martha closed the card and placed it on top of the journal. After blinking a few times, she picked up her wine glass and held it aloft.

"To you, Elizabeth White, and to Palmerston House."

The wine warmed and calmed her a little. Elizabeth and Keith had followed her suggestion all those years ago and approached Dorothy, who'd inherited their childhood home, but done nothing to maintain it. There had been a lot of work to do, but the couple embraced the challenge and from Elizabeth's occasional letters, opened it as a bed and breakfast property. Sadly, Keith had passed away not long after, leaving Elizabeth the legacy of their hard work and dreams.

Life was so unfair sometimes.

Martha gazed at the journal. Martha's Adventures. The fire inside burned a bit brighter and the sadness morphed into a slow sense of purpose. It was time to write. Not to be a world famous author, no, nothing of the sort. But time to revisit her life and cherish the important moments.

15

MEMORIES AND MEMOIRS

2009

Funny how the older one got, the more they think of the past. It was Dorothy's seventieth birthday. How had this lifetime sped by so fast? Martha's hand hovered above the phone. She longed to hear her big sister's voice again, to wish Dorothy many happy returns and pretend, for a while, they were close again.

Their last conversation still hurt Martha, when Dorothy blamed her for their mother's death. Perhaps if Dorothy had visited over the years, things might be different. They might still be sisters who laughed together and shared secrets.

It was late evening and winter was in full force. Martha walked away from the phone. In the cottage it was cold enough without risking Dorothy's icy response. She'd sent her a card, as she did every year, and like almost every preceding year, it would have to be enough.

After prodding the fire to ignite some warmth, Martha poured a sherry and returned to the kitchen table where a notebook was open. Elizabeth's journal was long since filled and this was the most recent in a series of large writing pads. Where she'd once kept her pendant in the box in the cupboard, she now stockpiled her words.

Each notebook represented either a time, or a place. Some crossed over. And she was almost up to date with what she secretly called her memoirs. There were big holes though and tonight reminded her so much of an early part of her life here in this beloved cottage.

One moment the wind was a gale, buffeting the cottage with icy air from the Atlantic Ocean with such power I feared the roof might come away. Then, silence. Abrupt, utter silence. This was my first winter in Ireland and I had serious doubts about my choice of destination. How I missed summer Christmas at Palmerston House, where the days were long and hot, and the house was filled with people. Here I was alone in a tiny cottage overlooking one of the coldest seas on the planet. When the wind didn't start howling again, I wrapped myself tightly in the blanket I'd been huddling beneath near the fireplace and drew back a curtain. At first, my mind couldn't comprehend what I saw. Instead of the matching, endless grey of sea and sky, I gazed upon an incredible sight. Soft white flakes fell onto the lawn, and as far as I could see. It was snowing. And it was Christmas Day.

Ah, what a wondrous introduction to winter on the Irish coast! But the snow fell until a thick blanket covered everything in sight. Martha had tried to bring more wood in as the temperatures plummeted, but struggled with depth of snow and wet wood. Thank goodness a thoughtful teacher dropped by with a small package of turkey and Christmas cake, and he helped clear a path and brought in enough logs to get her by.

It was a sharp lesson and one she learned from. Always have enough fuel for the fire, and always keep enough food in the cottage. Which was one of the reasons she'd worked so hard to grow her own produce and turn it into part of her sustainable larder.

How do I share these stories?

"Do I really want to?" she murmured aloud. There were some more...intimate memories in there. Nothing to make a person blush of course, rather it was the heartfelt recollection of the fondness she'd felt for Enrique and Aksel and other sweet men who'd been part of her journey through life.

Yet, nothing at all about the one man who still held her heart and always would. To write about Thomas Blake? Martha put down her pen and closed the notebook. Never. Not even one word, because words didn't matter. She pushed herself to her feet, more than ready for bed. A memory was at the edge of her mind and it was unwelcome.

Martha checked the front door was locked and turned off the lights. The wind from the Atlantic saturated the cottage with the scent of the sea and it was enough to break through the last of Martha's resistance. She sat on her bed with her eyes closed.

16

A PROMISE ON THE BEACH

1968

Warm, humid air surrounded Martha and hot sand burnt her feet. It was midnight in the middle of a fierce summer storm. Her clothes were damp from the sea and Thomas refused to let go of her arm.

She needed to run, to escape this terrible night. Because if she hesitated any longer, she'd stay.

"I'll wait for you. There," Thomas pointed to the sea, "at the end of the jetty, I will wait. Every day I will be there to meet the dawn, as we have done so many times. Promise you'll come back."

This was really happening. Martha glanced at the jetty which was almost submerged by powerful waves.

"Promise me!" Thomas insisted.

"Alright!" Martha cried out.

"No, Martha. A proper promise or it's not real. Say it."

"I promise! I promise I'll return, Tom! Now let me go!"

He did, and she ran blindly into the storm. Away from the pain, the betrayal, and her own stubbornness. His words followed her through the rain, declaring his love for her, yet still she'd flown across the beach to the stone steps.

17

MEMORIES AND MEMOIRS

2009

With a start, Martha opened her eyes. Her heartbeat thudded and she gripped the pendant so tightly it hurt. Not fair. She'd buried all this long ago.

Bit by bit she repacked the memory. Too far in the past to matter. Behind her. Part of what shaped her into the person she was now, so no regrets.

"I like who I am!"

Promises were broken all the time.

Martha undressed and slipped into bed. She pulled the blankets up around her face, shivering a little. Being alone wasn't so bad.

18

A CALL HOME

2017

Martha hobbled from the kitchen, cup of tea in one hand and cane in the other. Her ankle was heavily bandaged. Finally, she'd followed her doctor's advice and had the ankle operated upon. It would never be quite as good as the other, but now the nagging pain she'd been accustomed to was all but gone.

Every day was an improvement, which was just as well with winter about to make its appearance in force, and her lack of mobility wasn't getting the wood in or the last of the vegetables bottled. If not for the help from neighbours these past weeks, she'd be in deep trouble.

She lowered herself onto the sofa and rested the cane at her side. As she sipped her tea, she stared at the envelope propped against a small vase of late flowers. Dorothy's handwriting was a little different, not the firm strokes Martha knew, but her sister's writing nonetheless.

It wasn't her birthday. So why, after all these years, had Dorothy written a letter? With a small sigh, Martha put her teacup onto the table and opened the envelope.

Inside was one sheet of delicate paper.

Martha read it once, then stared into the distance. None of it made sense. Her hand holding the letter shook until she drew in a long, deep breath, and raised it again.

Dear Martha,

I have battled with myself over the wisdom of this letter. After all these years—this lifetime we have been apart—I ask myself if it is right to tell you what really happened that night...and in the days and months afterward. Will knowledge give you peace and let you put this to rest? Perhaps your absence from my life for almost half a century has been to protect yourself from finding out.

I am a coward to have waited until now when my life is so close to its end, but I cannot go to my grave with this burden. You see, I know the truth.

What truth? Martha already knew the truth. It was between her and Thomas, so why would Dorothy say there was more to it? And, as for absence! Who refused to come to their own parents' funerals?

You need to understand, I acted out of a desire to protect you from yourself. Mother and I had grown concerned by your poor choices, not only with the girls you called friends but the danger you insisted on placing yourself in with Thomas Blake. As if a man like him could ever be suitable for you! Yet you ignored our concerns and turned your back on our pleas, spending all your time with him. Mother was beside herself. Did you ever think for one moment of anyone other than yourself back then?

Mother feared for your future and often wrote; asking me to speak with you, reason with you about the boy. Of course, I knew that would be not only a waste of my time but quite likely hasten you into an unsuitable marriage. Thomas, after all, could not have been anything other than a rebellious fling, and Mother should have left things alone from the beginning.

What they should have done was both stayed out of it!

I should have stayed in the city, or left the country, anything other than come home for your engagement party. Mother refused to host the party or even attend, and I was terribly worried for her state of mind. All she ever wanted, Martha, was for you to finish your education and marry well. You need to understand she had nothing at all to do with the events we speak of now.

Martha creased her forehead. She'd never understood Mother's strange comments after Father died. Something about making a mistake about Thomas, that he was a good boy. And that things were never as they seem.

You were surprised I was there for your big night in the local hall. It was as though you did not know what to do with me, so you sent one of your friends to keep me company. She was quite the chatterbox about her feelings around your engagement and I found myself in the position to set the wheels in motion. To nudge you in the right direction.

None of this made sense. Martha knew exactly who Dorothy meant, but what did their conversation at Martha and Thomas' engagement party have to do with later events on the beach?

Please come to River's End, dear. Please come home and let us speak one more time. I would come to you, but my heart is not strong and travel is out of the question.

As always,

Dorothy

"Why now?" Martha ran a hand through her hair. Was Dorothy's health so bad she couldn't pick up a phone to discuss this? And why River's End? What possible reason was there to go now?

Rain pattered on the roof, then became a deluge. Always all or nothing here. It was November, and River's End would be warm. Long days and pleasant evenings. And Elizabeth to visit at Palmerston House.

Please come home and let us speak one more time.

Martha cupped the pendant in her hand.

"Of course I will, sister."

ABOUT THE AUTHOR

Phillipa lives just outside a beautiful town in country Victoria, Australia. She also lives in the many worlds of her imagination and stockpiles stories beside her laptop.

Apart from her family, Phillipa's great loves include music, reading, growing veggies, and animals of all kinds.

She loves hearing from readers and sends out a monthly email with news, competitions, author recommendations, and lots of other goodies.

www.phillipaclark.com